Henry Stevens

Poetry and rhymed jottings

Henry Stevens

Poetry and rhymed jottings

ISBN/EAN: 9783337261122

Printed in Europe, USA, Canada, Australia, Japan

Cover: Foto ©Andreas Hilbeck / pixelio.de

More available books at **www.hansebooks.com**

Poetry

AND

Rhymed Jottings,

BY

HENRY STEVENS,

(DIED 9TH MAY, 1887).

Bristol :—
LAVARS & CO., PRINTERS, BROAD STREET.
1890.

TO   THOSE   WHO   KNEW   HIM,

The following pages are dedicated.

The contents both grave and gay are such as have, from
time to time, been preserved by the
compiler of the book.   No care has been taken to exclude
trifles, which did not receive from the author
other than a moment's
thought, or to bring into prominence matter which
bears evidence of more careful consideration.

In the belief that many friends would take pleasure
in its perusal the present
collection is now issued in book form.

THE ROAD TO RUIN.

[Suggested by Frith's exquisite Pictures.]

———o———

DRAW back the curtain, see the trembling light
That heralds day, is glimmering in the east.
Long has the orgie been, at last when brains
Were hot with wine, the cards were wily brought
And he just freed from bondage—as he deemed—
With all the golden fruits of non-age heaped.
His wealth of lands, must in flushed triumph see
The hectic, fleeting pageant, men call life.

Could no good angel guard him in that hour,
When soft as angels' breathings morning broke,
Speak of his home amid ancestral trees,
The terraces alive with summer flowers,
The fountains loosening silver to the sky,
The giant Lebanon cedars on the lawn ;
What ! barter these, for this ?

No angel spake, but rather devils cried,
"Our host has lost : we'll give him his revenge.
Close up the curtains, bring more lights," and he,
The gilded fool, wavered awhile, and then
The stakes are doubled, trebled—higher play,
"More wine," " Ho, ho," the leering devils mocked.
What saw the sun a little later on ?
A youthful face, but haggard, as with age,
And whitened lips, that formed a stifled oath,
The first step on the road to ruin trod.

But two swift summers sped, and alien feet
Are treading gardens, terraces, and hall :
And other owners stride the teeming fields
That once were his : but his, ah, never more.

A grand stroke this : sure fortune must at last
Smile on him now.
                    Our Isthmian games are on.
The broad blue riband of the turf
Dazzles a thousand longing eyes, and he,
Urged by the semi-devil at his side,
Whose vulture-clutch is on his shoulder gripped,
Who whispers with those stern satanic lips
"Take, take ; I know, I know ;"
And speaks with honied tongue,
And swears that all shall be recovered
" Be you bold enough." " No more, no more ;
What if I fail ?" " You cannot fail ;" and so
His book is made.

As in a dream he stands
And gazes on the levelled turf below,
Trim and smooth-shaven as a garden lawn ;
As in a dream he hears the surging notes
Of thrice ten thousand voices hoarsely cry
" The start is made."
As in a dream he sees
Kaleidoscopic colors thundering past ;
As in a dream is heard the thunderous thud
Of horses, mad as riders, for the goal.
Minutes are ages now.
Another roar
From full-lunged voices so the first, is faint,
As but the lisping of a summer sea
Against a shelving rock
He dared not look;
Nor need he.   In his mentor's face he saw
All he need see, and in the lurid sky,
And from the seething, maddened crowd below
Came, Ruin, ruin.   Lost, lost, lost.

So far, the muttering of the storm, but now
The crash of hopeless ruin.
She, his wife,
Starts to his side, and all her beauty blanched
With a great terror, murmurs, " Dearest say
What mean these men ?"   He whispers in her ear,
And she, half dazed, looks wondrously ; and then,
" Oh no, no, no, not that ! I never knew,"
She cried.

Then faltered, bravely keeping back her tears
Lest she unman him.   E'en the sorry knaves,
Who've but to work the cold law's stern behest,
Are moved by trembling lips and broken tones,
And pass into the ante-room, where now
The liveried lackeys discount coming doom,
And each top each in speedy care of self.

" What ruin, perfect ruin ?" he is dumb,
But draws her to him, " Oh, I will be brave ;
And yet," then tears that will not be restrained,
Arms round his neck, her face hid on his breast,
" And all must go ?" he gravely answered, " All."

She stood alone.
Her pride had been in home, and all of home.
The many gifts upon her bridal tour
Are hers no longer ; all the jewels bought,
In the long glittering Corso out of Rome,
The rich robes wrought by cunning Genoese.

Mosaics of the Florentines' proud art,
Rich gauds from Naples.

        Scarce a city seen
But proffered proofs of his then lavish love:
All hers no longer—hers, ah never more.
Her tear-blurred eyes saw ruin stark and blank.
A long, low wail of women's anguish smote
The summer night,
A face of woe looked upward to the stars.

     *   *   *   *

A wretched room, the pinch of want about,
The plaster dropping from the mildewed walls,
All of past splendours dwindled down to this.
A baby's wail half soothed by baby nurse,
The mistress of the house seeking her due;
Well, well, it is her right, just as my lord
From broad fat acres claims his legal rents.

A sweet low pleading, and the pale sad face
Dissolves all rancour; " Yes, yes I will wait,"
And so she passed.
" Wait, and for what, we have no hope," he cried,
" I've written, written, written, aye to all
The butterflies that in my golden days
Were loud in mouthing friendships, now I plead
For aid, replies fall fast enough, but none
Heed our hard wants, it is, ' Rents are to be paid,'
' Our home demands *are* frightful,' ' Wish you well,'
' And shall be *so* glad when the times improve.'
A hundred echoes to the the self-same tune."
Here his voice faltered—scanty food,
The wretched housing—all his spirits broke.
He, leaning on the table, fairly wept.
"Come, come," she cried, "who is the strongest now?
Look, darling here, whilst you have been at work
I have been working too—see here, and here."
He looked at her: a few poor, pretty views,
Such as our friends may praise
When praise is all that's needed; when, as now,
The huge gaunt wolf of want bays at the door
Sops, such as these, are feebleness itself.

She had yet to learn this lesson, and she passed
Into the night, the city was aflame
With million lights, a scent of rain
Was in the air, she drew her scant shawl close—
Not this the ermined well-furred robe of old,
When erst she sought the city marts, her steeds,
Well groomed, and corn-fed, at her lackey's bid
Backed on their steaming haunches, and were near

Half hid in hammer cloth, obsequious then,
The bowing heads, 'mid these she queenly passed.
And now a shrinking woman shows her wares,
And pleads for purchase. "No, no, no, not now,"
"The market's overstocked," "there's no demand
For such as these;" and ever such repulse,
And ever, in her ear, these parrot-cries.

One vulgar wretch who lumbering, sleepy looked,
And left his thumb-mark on the fairest sketch,
Offered for all what might have bought a meal.
"Well! well! he didn't want them"
Whistled in contempt, slunk to his lair again, and she—
—A woman's anger burned in woman's face.

"Enough, enough," she moaned, "my cup is full."

A heavy rain was falling, as she passed
Back to her sordid home, the crazy stairs
Creaked to her footstep. Which her room?
Ah, this! She hardly dare to turn
The rusty handle; oh! thank God.
                              He slept.
The babes had wailed themselves to sleep,
The fire had dwindled out. The rising wind
Blew gusts of rain against the papered panes.
Worn and exhausted, hunger fought with sleep,
Sleep was at last the victor, and she slept.

Close fast the door!
                    And close out all this world.
He lifts his arm unto the sullen night,
Which hot and sulphurous is fast settling down,
A murmur of low thunder speaks of storm.
Far off, and dulled by distance, tolls a passing bell;
Fit sound—fit echo to his mad despair.
Despair has trampled hope, and heralds death,
And nerves his hand unto the final deed.
'Tis done! and wildly through the shattered door,
White faces look with horror on the dead.
What of him now? rude coffin, pauper's grave;
His requiem, falling rain and falling leaves.

Close, close, oh record of a wasted life.

SPRING.

LIGHT and shadows interlace,
Smiles and tears are on thy face,
Thou, whose early crown is set,
Rich with scented violet.

Summer hold a fuller blushing,
Deeper crimson Autumn dyes,
But the hopes with spring time flushing,
To its blue and white fleck'd skies.

Give a promise, give a glow,
Sunnier hours may never know,
Soft the sower sows the seed
That shall to the harvest lead.

Thine, the tender leaflet budding
All about our lattice panes ;
Thine, the early star-flower studding,
Fern-hid banks in winding lanes.

Thine, the morning's silv'ry haze,
Thine, the wealth of spangled dew,
Thine, the lark's delirious lays,
Drown'd and lost in ether's blue.

Light and life on all our ways,
Bring thou in our golden days,
Soft the sower sows the seed
That shall to the harvest lead.

AT THE GARDENS.

" THE Conservatives' flag," cried a man, as a blue
  And emblazoned rich banner rose proudly in sight:
" *Flag*," said another, " be hanged if we do !"
  And I looked round and thought that the second
    was right.

LEIGH WOODS.

OLD Woods of Leigh!—old Woods of Leigh!
  Your praises have been sung
By many a nobler harp than mine,
  By many a gifted tongue.
And well dost thou deserve each song
  That hath been sung of thee;
Thou'rt linked with many a pleasant hour,
  Oh, waving Woods of Leigh!
Your corners, where the lichens grow—
  Your rocks, that ivies creep—
Your fair, tall trees, that gaily crown
  The summit of the steep—
All, all are hallowed to mine eyes,
  For there loved feet have trod,
And song and shout rang bravely out
  Across thy dark green sod.
And loving eyes have on me shone,
  And dim seemed worldly wars
When o'er thy solemn woods were thrown
  The gentle light of stars.

A glorious spectacle art thou
  When morning interweaves,
The rich red glory of its sun
  Amidst thy world of leaves.
And well I love to tread thy paths,
  With measured step and slow,
When in the west the setting sun
  Is gently sinking low,
Or out in summer-haunted time
  To linger in thy dells,
And catch the low sweet under chime
  Of far-off Sabbath bells.
And mind how oft in youth-time we
  Through thy paths leapt along,
And how the music of each heart
  Kept pace with wild bird song.

     *   *   *   *

The sun flames now o'er field and croft,
  The sward is rich with many dyes,
The summer breezes—balmy—soft—
  Recall a thousand memories:
A thousand thoughts of bud and bloom,
  The heather's hue, the tangled dell,
The deep, dark glen, within whose gloom,
  So cloister-like, we loved to dwell,

And plucking from the glade the flowers,
　Called forth by the light voice of May,
Then did we deem this world of ours
　Had no more care than summer's day.
There stands the hill—there lies the brook—
　And there the Avon's winding stream—
And there the tree o'er-shadowed nook,
　Where hath been woven many a dream ;
But where are those, the tried and true
　Who first our souls' communings knew ?

Alas, they are not !—Time hath been
　By us, and swiftly sped away
And some who cheered life's fitful scene,
　Are sleeping 'neath their load of clay ;
And some are in another land,
　Have kindred in another clime.
Alas ! the whole of that bright band,
　Are severed by the lapse of time.
Nor song of birds from every spray,
　Nor e'en the mellow south wind's tone
Can chase sad thoughts from us away,
As, on this gentle summer day,
　We tread thy paths—alone !

CHILDREN AT PLAY.

THE old room echoes with children's feet,
　And they climb the old man's chair ;
And his waning pulses must quicker beat
　As he looks on each bright brow there.
Gleam Marion's curls with a golden hue,
　Dear Kate's are as swart as night,
Sweet Alice's eyes are the sky's sweet blue,
　Shine Maud's with a deeper light.
The air is scented with summer flowers,
　Just kissed by the twilight low,
And night is setting her starry dowers
　To welcome the May moon's glow.
Play on in your beauty—fair young girls,
　Play on in your childish glee ;
And rippled in light, let your blended curls
　Fall fair on your grandsire's knee.
And as childhood dallies with age's gloom,
　He cries as they round him creep :
" *Oh, bother the brats, get out of the room,*
　Don't you see that I want to sleep."

TO THE PORTRAIT OF A LADY OF THE SEVENTEENTH CENTURY.

GLEAM in thy beauty from our walls—
  Each touch is glorious yet—
Thou cam'st to us from stately halls,
  In grand old Somerset.
For years thy fathers held the soil,
  And thought their equals none ;
Nor dreamt that armed with trading spoil
  At last would enter one
Who passed with scorn the blazoned shields
  Of all thine honoured line ;
And, striding through the teeming fields,
  Said proudly " These are mine.
To all the winds past legends blow,
  I've bought these lands, and thus
I'll found a county name."   And so
  Thou cam'st at last to us,
But bring'st no hint, no thought, no trace
  Of life, of death, of birth,
But bear'st the undefined grace
  Of foremost ones of earth.
What joys in life's swift shifting march
  Brought sorrows in their train,
Oh, thou beneath some silvering larch
  Two hundred summers lain ?
That is, if English daisied sod
  Thy winsome beauty's fed,
Or sleep'st in steepled house of God,
  Midst centuries' charnelled dead.
Thou'st fretted, fumed, plucked roses, burrs,
  But found with all, at last,
Our heaviest hours are gossamers
  When once those hours are passed.
Say, hadst thou earnest work to do,
  When King and Crown in check,
Stern Cromwell and his rebel crew
  The race won by a neck ?
Say, when our land at length released
  From clutch of crop-eared carles,
When England rocked with wine and feast,
  Did'st welcome Royal Charles ?
Say, did'st thine ears with horror shut,
  Did pity brim thine eyes,
When Jefferys strode thy county glut
  With blood of Red Assize ?

Still silent ?— gazing from thy frame
A monumental stone !
The eve is rich with sunset's flame,
And autumn's chill winds moan ;
So winter's storms will vengeance wreak,
So summers gild the bough,
When we who idly dream and speak
Shall grow as dumb as thou.

THE VACANT COT.

SWEETEST dream of life—dispelled
This last week—our baby held.
Other voices in the air,
Other children everywhere.
Not for us ; and sorrow rests,
Graven ever, on our breasts
Not for him—the worldly race,
Not for him—the pride of place.
All our glory, all our pride,
In the simple words—he died.

Those who cannot fathom say ;
"Well, he early passed away."
Had they prayed for baby's sake ?
Had they known the long, dull ache ?
Our hearts leapt at faintest glow
When a gleam of life would show.
Did they know our household blank
When that life for ever sank ?
Those who cannot fathom say ;
"Well, he early passed away."

Past all hopes, and past all schemes,
We had woven in our dreams.
Seen him, clad in hope and truth,
Battling life, with glow of youth.
Crowned with coming summers, when
He would stand a man with men.
All our hopes. of bud and bloom,
Garnered now in baby's tomb ;
All our glory, all our pride,
In the simple words—he died.

ITALY.

———

WAS it a dream, or did we really go
To fairest Genoa? Saw from out the sea
Her marble palaces, her stately domes arise,
And melting to their watching crown of hills,
Clasped with the blue of her unclouded skies—
Felt all the power that through all pulses thrill
When touched by peerless beauty? Through her
    streets
E'er leaning seaward, rich with light and life,
In grand old fanes, amid the gorgeous glooms
That haunt them ever; court-yards thickly filled
With orange blooms that scented earth and air.

Did we pass on from here to Pisa?
Saw from out the earth her leaning tower,
Lit with the glow of an Italian moon—
Her Campo Santo filled with holy earth?
Did we pass through all the glories of the teeming
    land,
'Till in the night in cloudscape shone the fires
That spake the advent of Imperial Rome?

Oh! grandest fane that ever rose from earth!
Oh! fountains wooing ever sun or moon!
Oh! ruins with your mystic memories crowned!
Oh! tawny river winding through them all!

Still, if a dream, away we seemed to glide,
And in the wane of an Italian noon
Saw Naples looming, and, above, the cloud
That broods for ever on the lava'd heights
Of the volcanic mount; and later on
The shimmering fires that spake of slumbering power,
In tremulous glories, lit the falling night.

A dream of morning flooding all the earth!
A dream of sunlight on the bluest waves!
Crowned Naples sinks behind us, and beyond
Rises fair Capri. Do we float
Into huge grottoes, where an azure light
Is ever haunting, and phosphorent gleams
That shame the radiance of a summer moon?

Now deep mid-arching vines and orange groves,
And plucking fruit from every teeming branch—
Is this Sorrento?

Ah! a fleeting dream
Of scented trees that bent to kiss the waves,
And towering high above us caught the light
Of stars and moon?

Ah! pass—light hearted band,
Who touched the source of laughter, but whose songs,
Plaintive as moan of wind on Autumn eve,
Gave moisture to our eyelids.   Then rang out
Some rippling peal, and thus ran light, ran shade,
As sun and cloud across the harvest field.

A dream of ruins—
Hollow shells, that once held pomp and pride and
     power,
Now staring blank across the sunny plains,
The chafe of rope is on the dry well's side,
The chafe of lips that drank from bubbling fount.
Two thousand years, and yet the chariot wheels
Running through all her highways, show their scars,
Two thousand years—still in the marts of wine
The marble holds the stain of reeking cup;
Two thousand years—the bread is here, the fruit
Plucked for the rich man's feast, and on the walls
The glow of form and colour gleams out bright
And lustrous through two thousand summers dead
Through miles of molten lava weird and quaint,
Titanic form that seem to guard the mount,
Grotesque, fantastic—All our wildest dreams
Fade into summer lispings!

Say the seas,
In fiercest madness suddenly were froze,
Bound to eternal silence; these the shapes
That pile up-up the swart, scarred mountain side
Is it a dream—the yawning sulphurous depths,
The cruel mountain yearning to be free?
So back to Naples in the gathering gloom.

A festa's held, and dancers dance, and song
And music are about and up the bay.
The waves are lapping and the rush
Of molten fires is leaping to the sky,
Raining to earth, in thousand varied hues:
Whilst over all this life the mountain stands,
One awful menace ever on his lips,
So life so death are ever side by side.

City of flowers, and flower of cities, thou:
Well art thou named, sweet Florence.

Cool arcades
Hold white-limbed statues, waiting breath of life.
Thy poet's spell is on thee, sun and flowers
Thy gifts for ever; in our dream we pass
Up heights where rain of flush of roses blow
Thicker than daisies in our colder land.
A dream of palaces beyond compute,
Of miles of paintings flashing from their walls ;
Of thick-housed bridges o'er the Arno's stream ;
Of tender lights that through the woodlands crept ;
Of grand mosaics wanting naught but life ;
Of stately tombs where proud Florentines sleep—
Thy poet's statue watching over all.
Pearl of the world ! City of flowers,
And flower of all cities, proudly stand.

Where do we drift ?
A city mystic, silent, grand.
Are we enchanted ? scent of sea and seaweeds floating
On the liquid green ; towers, palaces, and domes are
    all about,
And everywhere the deep, eternal sea.

This strangest dream of all !
Of towers that leap three hundred feet above ;
Of churches filled to faintness with perfume ;
Of noisome dungeons far below the waves ;
Of round moons gloating over broad lagoons ;
Of sullen deeps where death to throw a net ;
Of burnished shrines that blur the glow of sun ;
Of huge bronzed giants clashing out the hours ;
Of marts, throat-filled with gems of either Ind ;
Of twelve fair brides, girt with Imperial glow ;
Of argosies of gold cleaving the waves ;
Of proudest Doges, wedding land to sea.

Venice uncrowned, but ever Venice still—
Home of all arts, theme of ten thousand songs—
Each pulse beats to thee, from our cold grey land.
Venice uncrowned, but ever Venice still.
So Milan passes, with her fretted dome,
Her gates, her palaces, her stately ways.
So are these hours—in Dreamland—gone and past,
And through the mist of tenderest April days
Come out to greet us, well beloved, at last,
Two words with magic circled—England, Home !

CHATTERTON.

THE dying sun gleamed red on Redcliff pile,
Kissing the windows' many-coloured pane,
Throwing a dreamy light on nave and aisle,
On monument and tomb an azure stain ;
And, ere these glories into night did wane,
There strayed a youth into that holy place,
And many thoughts seemed sweeping o'er his brain,
Of hazy beauty and of half-formed grace,
Which on that pile and in that hour it seemed his joy
    to trace.

He gazed upon each richly sculptured arch,
Each carven column—statue grim and lone—
He, through the windows, saw the young moon march
Her gentle ray upon the fair fane thrown,
Made shadows seem as substance—senseless stone
Grow dim, unearthly—in that solemn light
Some would have been affrighted, but the tone
Of that boy's spirit revelled in the night,
She was a monitor to him, and much he owned her
    might.

For he was CHATTERTON—the young boy-bard—
Conning high themes beneath the holy night,
His ardent hopes then shew that high reward
E'er waits on genius ; did he deem aright ?
Answer ye many, who beneath the blight
Of cold neglect, have shrunk and passed away.
It's but the flower in bloom that meets our sight
And glads us with its radiance : who shall say
How many seeds lie dead beneath the uncaring clay ?

          *   *   *   *   *   *

He mounted stairs—he stood on Redcliff roof,
The night was all unclouded, and the sky,
Gemmed with the moon and stars, like sable woof,
Flashing with jewels—with a poet's eye,
He saw this lustre, all was silent by,
And long he gazed upon the high heavens, when
A star shot all across them glitteringly
It blazed, pure, bright, a single instant—then
'Twas darkened—it returned to realms unknown to
    men.

Thy life, oh, Chatterton, was like that star!
Gemmed with a lustre all too bright to last;
Too soon death came—self summoned—and did mar
Thy genius, which so mighty was and vast,
And should have sojourned with us—not have passed,
As passed the star, into a fearful gloom;
But should have lit us longer, and have cast
A brighter ray, nor just served to illume
The darkened way which led thee to despair, death,
    and thy tomb.

TWO DREAMS.

JUST in the dim and mystic hour, ere yet
The day had yielded to the foot of night,
And of the two was gentle twilight born,
I had a dream, and in my vision saw,
As in a mirror pictured.

PEACE.

The waves were falling on the sloping beach,
The corn fast ripening on the swelling cliff;
Far out at sea ships with their snowy sails
Were forging chains of commerce which should bind
Far nations in the closest links to ours.
I looked across the teeming land,—I saw
A thousand victories were thine, oh Peace:
Schools built, well filled and earnest men afoot
To combat with the plague-spots of the time;
And marshy heaths, redeemed from fen and fog,
Spake with their yellow breasts of ripening food;
And valleys spanned with bridges, over which
Panted the swift steam-engine, by its side
The flashing wire that laughs at limping time;
And want and crime were dying fast;
For I saw well-paid Labour in the land,
And Education with it hand in hand—
And where these are then Want and Vice soon die.
The world had reached a better time;—who wrote
And touch'd the nation's pulses had his meed:
A crown to him who gave near life to stone—
A crown to him who made the canvas breathe.
No need for men to die that deeds may live,
For shouts fall coldly on a corpse's ear,
And find no echo in the quiet grave.

Such was the time that in my dream I saw,
And as I looked, from mine and forge I heard—
From schools, from railroad, from ships out at sea—
From cities purged of taint of foul disease—
From stately buildings rising through the land—
A chorus of invisible voices cry,
" Ten thousand victories are thine, oh Peace!"
So that dream pass'd; then through the blurring mist
Another vision rose :—I saw before me

WAR

A fearful scene it was of rack and woe,
Of armed navies beating down on shores,
Of strange men fiercely pouring through the streets,
No spot so holy but was now defiled ;
What Peace had raised up, War had overthrown.

I heard the bells peal wildly out " To arms!"
The drums' fierce roll re-echoing the cry.
Night was upon the city—night, and War
Roared its hoarse summons even at her gates,
And hurried faces spake of hope to those
Who wildly clung, and did not dare to hope—
Faces that ere the morn stared blank at heaven,
And mocked with stony looks the rising sun.

Alas! alas! and in my dream I saw
The midnight skies with burning cities red,
And God's own image hack'd and hew'd, and blood
Poured as a ghastly wine out on the earth.
I heard the orphan's wail, the widow's moan —
I saw blank places at the board and hearth,
The corn unsickled, rotting in the fields,
The smouldering ruin where the homestead stood.

Then that dream died, but thought bred thought,
And long I mused, and prayed that our
Dear ocean Pearl inviolate may be
That rulers of her councils yet shall hold
Amid the foremost nations of the earth,
Our England's name untarnished ; that I saw
Within the compass of my troubled dream
No fitful shadows of a coming time.

LITTLE MAMIE'S DEAD.

RING de bell dat tolls de knell,
  Humbly bow de head,
Heavy dis, de hour has fell :
  Little Mamie's dead.
Nebber more I see her dance,
  Or jump on daddy's knee,
What um care, now dat her glance,
  Am ever lost to me.

            Ring de bell that tolls de knell,
              Humbly bow de head ;
            Heavy dis, de hour has fell :
              Little Mamie's dead.

Jus' last week, in cotton croft,
  Wus um singing low ;
Warbling pure, and warbling soft,
  Ah! 'twas dis I know—
Dat her songs, too good for us :
  Angels from de dome,
Envied us her songs, and thus
  Called little Mamie home.

            Ring de bell dat tolls de knell,
              Humbly bow de head ;
            Heavy dis, de hour has fell :
              Little Mamie's dead.

Ah! de sorrow, much, ah! sore,
  Ah! de loss of sweet ;
Nebber more on Cabin floor,
  Comes pat of little feet.
What am sunshine, what am flowers,
  An' Mamie nebber by,
You hev yours, but all of ours
  Am vanished from our sky.

            Ring de bell dat tolls de knell,
              Humbly bow de head ;
            Heavy dis, de hour has fell ·
              Little Mamie's dead.

QUEEN SQUARE.

(AT A TORCHLIGHT DEMONSTRATION).

I thought, as gazing on the scene,
  In all its civic phases,
When Governments on torches lean,
  They're going, sure, to blazes.

TWO SONNETS.

I.—LOVE'S FIRST GIFT.

IT was the time of sun, and wealth of flowers,
Fair summer thou wert with us then,
And hill and woodland, field, and croft and glen
Were hallowed by thy thousand welcome dowers.
The sky was like our hopes, unshrouded,
Pure as wert thou my only earthly shrine;
The future seemed as glowing as unclouded.
And when I placed upon that hand of thine
A simple ring, just taken from my finger,
How sweet thy looks, how soft and low thy tone,
And there entranced, with deep thoughts did we linger
Until the light of day had nearly flown;
But with the flush of joy upon our way—
What reck'd we of the fading light, the evening calm
    and gray?

II.—THE PICTURE.

I stood before a glowing picture, one
Pourtraying life and beauty, bud and bloom;
Others were hung around that room—
And all were rich with many lights, but none
Could equal this—a young and laughing girl,
Crown'd with a coronal of summer flowers;
Her parted lips revealed a wealth of pearl,
Neck, cheek, and brow rejoiced in nature's dowers.
One snow-white arm was softly, coyly raised,
On it was perched a plumaged bird, whose beak
Turned as to fondle with her wooing cheek;
She seemed to wait for life, and long I gazed,
And turned away, and did not dare to speak,
Her beauty raised a dream I almost feared to break!

AT THE TURKISH BATHS.

STAMPED out by Harry Eighth, the bold,
    Forgotten by our sires,
Once more in College Green behold
    Ye Saynte Augustine *Fryers*.

TO LITTLE NELL.

PURE, amid things impure, thou wert a child
Too good for earth, and thy young heart
Knew much of sorrow, yet was ever mild,
To all, but most to him, who bore a part,
With all thy suff'rings, felt with thee each smart,
Yet when his soul rejoiced, thou could'st be gay,
As ever child released from school or holiday.

To prop, and cheer, the waning lamp of age,
Thy soul a woman's, link'd to childhoods brow,
Was the high task, thou fear'st not to engage,
And blessing rest, upon thy soul, for thou,
Wast taught by nature, never lore of sage ;
Did ever tell, unto thy brave heart, how,
To combat, with the world, and worldly things
Untainted, and high soul'd, midst all thy sufferings.

And when at length, thou found'st a place of rest,
Just in thine opening spring, and life's first bloom !
Thou turn'st away from where all souls are blest,
Thou found'st a refuge in thy narrow tomb.
Dark, noisome, yet a happy resting place,
To those like thee, who bow to meet His will,
Who leaving earthly homes, find homes of grace.
Peace to thy ashes! slumber softly, still
It grieves us, those should live, and work us ill,
And sow dissension, discord, strife, whilst they
The young, the pure high soul'd are first to pass away.

THIRTY SEVEN.

AH ! the years have fleeted by
As though mirrored in a dream,
And I little cared, as I
Floated, floated with the stream ;
But I've paused awhile to-day,
For a passing glance has told,
Raven hairs are waxing gray,
And that I am growing old.

Ah ! how swift the seasons went,
How they hurried by, how soon
Frailest flowers of Spring were blent
With the full red rose of June ;
Ruddier Autumn's gorgeous touch
Gave its glories to the land ;
Swift as light the Winter's clutch
Shook them, shook them from my hand.

MORNING IN THE CITY.

MORNING breaks upon the city
  Fresh and pure, and calm and cool;
Not a wave of eager commerce
  Stirs as yet our civic pool.
Blows the free May air, untainted
  By the belch of grimy fires;
Sharp and clear up to the ether
  Rise now all our hundred spires.
Night has shed its coolest cisterns,
  Early dawn has to the town
Brought faint scent of far-off woodland,
  Blent with hint of breezy down;
And in ways that shall be trodden
  Soon with Mammon's hungriest greed,
Lo! with sunshine on its pinions,
  A white pigeon swoops to feed.

Early sunlight! lengthened shadows
  O'er the year-stained headstones creep,
In the tiny span—God's acre—
  Where the past old burghers sleep.
On each hand the rippling waters
  Gliding our dear city through
From the glories of the azure
  Give it back a brighter blue.
Venice-like the rippling vista,
  Heavy swathed with folded sails,
And blue hazes in the distance
  Gently robe the merchant bales.
From the towers above the cloisters
  Clear the early matins ring;
Gleam the grand old elms about them
  With the fresh full flush of Spring.

TUESDAY, Nov. 17, 1868.

I saw huge civic evils wrought—
  The wrecks, the consternation—
And musing to myself I thought,
  This *is* a *demons*-tration.

ON THE DEATH OF

GEORGE THOMAS,

December 14, 1869.

———

OUR loss is new, not less a mighty loss—
  So lately moving in our city ways
  The grand old form that all men loved to praise—
Listless the hand which scattered gold as dross.

He might have grasped our topmost civic crown,
  Have pleaded for us in Imperial halls;
  Yet fearing kindlier duties warped with thralls,
He wisely, nobly, trod ambition down.

Pass, reverend head, pass to thy narrow tomb—
  A golden link lost from our common weal;
  Thine not the honours won by clash of steel,
Yet better soldier girt not sword nor plume.

A warrior, aye, on want and foul disease,
  With open hand, with heart as well as tongue,
  He rallying others, proud defiance flung—
Christ send us champions such as these!

When snarling faction stirred the civic pool,
  And blatant rang the wildest passions out,
  Amid the storm, the tumult, and the shout,
He stood unmoved, collected, calm and cool.

And there and then upon the brawlers fell
  His shrewd, keen wit, his touch of nimble sense:
  The kindly smile, the native eloquence
So often used, but ever just and well.

Ah! well for him—from commerce reaping gain—
  Who leant on honour as a'biding staff,
  And claimed of right the proudest epitaph:
" His civic record knew not blot nor stain."

Honoured, beloved, he bowed to the behest.
  Mourn, mighty city; on each crowded way
  Silence and shadows fall. Behold, to-day,
A good man passes to his final rest!

SONG OF
THE CHRISTMAS CAROL SINGERS.

———

THE winter wind is blowing chill,
  The night is dark and bleak ;
We fold our garments closer still,
  It blanches each wan cheek.
We see your log illumined pane,
  We hear the voice of mirth ;
Ah, what care ye for wind or rain,
  As, seated round the hearth,
To each well-loved and honoured guest
  A welcome cup ye drink.
The wailing blast yields but a zest,
  Ah, gentles, pause and think.

    With no less joy would rise the din
      Or duller be the shout,
     If, from your store of wealth within,
      You lightened want without.

No doubt your rooms are very fair,
  And decked with rosy glow,
Our homes are bare, and every air
  Of heaven therein may blow.
Ah, mothers, as ye watch the light
  Play on each blossom's brow.
Think of us in this bitter night,
  Nor turn ye from us now ;
For far our wand'ring feet have strayed
  To sing our little rhyme—
Our simple Christmas carol, made
  More holy by the time.

    And no less joy will glad the din,
      Or duller be the shout,
     If, from your store of wealth within,
      You lighten want without.

TO AN ABSENT FRIEND.

I'M sitting all alane, my friend,
   An my heart is sick and sore,
For I hear na your guid voice, my friend,
   Nor your footstep on the floor ;
No footsteps on the floor, my friend,
   Tho' the year is on the wane,
And I thocht to see ye lang ere this—
   Oh, when will ye come again ?

Oh, lang's the winter's nicht my friend,
   And cald, and mirk, and drear,
For I miss the merry laugh, my friend,
   That was wont the nicht to cheer ;
That was wont the nicht to cheer, my friend,
   And I'm haunted by the strain
Of the last sweet sang ye sung to me—
   Oh, when will ye come again ?

Your chair is opposite, my friend,
   But the chair is yet unfilled,
My hame fire bleezes bright my friend,
   But to me its warmth seems chilled ;
Its very warmth seems chilled, my friend,
   Tho' it lichts the window pane,
As it used to licht ye through the byre—
   Ah, when will ye come again ?

The draught-board leans to the wall, my friend,
   Untouched the men may be,
For there's naebody noo i' the nicht, my friend,
   To play a game with me ;
To play a game with me, my friend,
   And laugh if his men were ta'en,
And be ane o' the few above Fortune's frowns—
   Oh, when will ye come again ?

Do ye mind our Autumn walks, my friend,
   How we read amang the sheaves
The books which are with me noo, my friend,
   But I daur na touch their leaves ;
I daur na touch their leaves, my friend,
   For I feel a thrill of pain,
And I'm lanesome noo in the winter's nicht—
   Oh, when will ye come again ?

CHRISTMAS.

LET the north wind, shrill and shrewdly,
  Pipe across the open moor,
Let it bluster, fierce and rudely,
  'Gainst the window, 'gainst the door;
Laugh we at its maddest yearning,
  For the evening lamps are lit,
And the Christmas log is burning,
  As it e'er should burn, and it
Throws its flame in deep recesses,
  Where the berries and the leaves
Clothe each nook in bravest dresses—
  Glistening gaily, interweaves
Pillar, arch, and round each rafter
  Twines it lovingly and bright,
Oh let bursts of jocund laughter
  Shake each gleaming leaf to-night,
For old Christmas is a fellow
  Every one should love, and he
Hath a laugh that's ever mellow,
  And a look that's full of glee.

Hark! the old church bells are pealing
  Out their soft melodious chime,
Thrilling hearts with joyous feeling
  Ever at this merry time,
Brightly eyes are beaming on us—
  Loving words from loving lips—
May the gleams that light upon us,
  Never know a dark eclipse.
Let the headed wine-cup glisten
  In the yule log's glorious light,
Loving eyes are bent, ears listen
  To our bravest songs to-night;
Wreathe the flying hours with pleasure,
  Christmas lends its social zest,
Music! strike your lightest measure,
  Let us foot it with the rest--
For old Christmas is a fellow
  Every one should love, and he
Hath a laugh that's ever mellow,
  And a look that's full of glee.

WRITTEN IN ILLNESS.

I gaze upon the woodlands and the full glow
  Of the bright sun is resting on the lea;
A flush of beauty haunts the world, and lo,
  Swift by my casement darts the busy bee,
The birds are carolling their notes of glee,
    And fair wild flowers from out the earth are
      springing,
And deep within yon dark woods, I see
    Fair children's forms—their light-toned voices
      ringing
Upon the air, devoid of earthly ill,
    Whilst here, by sickness pent, I lie calm motion-
      less, and still,

Yet sight, thank God, is left me still to look
  Out on the glossy woods and to espy,
Amid the leafy wilderness, a nook,
  Where when, as now, the summer sun shone high,
'Twas a delight, half listlessly, to lie
  With spirits of the olden time communing
Whilst the tall trees did shade the arid sky,
  And from glens far away the wild birds tuning,
Upon my ear fresh in its beauty fell,
    None happier then than I, in that half-shaded
      dell

Oh, worldly lovers! haply ye may vaunt
  Of the rich homes—the palaces of men—
But dearer far to me was my old haunt,
  Within the deep recesses of the glen,
On meek eyed eves of summer season, when
  The moon did look upon the woods and woo them,
With its coy glance of silent beauty, then
    'Twas a delight and love to wander through them
With step e'er solemn, tranquil, hushed and slow,
    Communing with the thoughts such hours doth
      nurse and know.

Thou, who in justice chasteneth, oh! let
  Thy rod fall lightly on me, and the glow
Of health again illumine me, and set
  Aside the weariness that haunts me now,
Oh, ease the throbbing of this feverish brow!
  Let me in joy look on the tall trees waving,
Let me rejoice in the glad brooklets' flow,
  The pleasant corn fields and the meadows laving!
Strong has the conflict been—let it be o'er
    And I arise and worship Thee amid Thy works
      once more.

SUNSET FROM PENPOLE POINT.

THE red sun, fast sinking in the west,
Has piled a burnished glory full and deep,
Such as should light a monarch to his rest,
And croft and woodland, vale and shore, and steep,
And the glad waves that in the distance leap,
Shine in the lustre of its dying might.
Now closer fall the shadows, earth dews weep,
The evening star grows brighter and more bright,
The fisher's lonely sail gleams clear against the
    coming night.

But ere the day hath hardly quailed, whilst yet
A glow of lingering glory haunts the sky:
Sweet is the seal upon the soft hour set,
When the low twilight silently droops nigh,
And the tall woodlands that are brooding by,
With deeper shadows, take a soberer dress;
When through the green lanes gentle night winds
    sigh,
Kissing sweet flowers in many a leaf'd recess,
Dear is the twilight hour to me with all its loneliness

Sweet would it be to linger, but we turn
And through the woodpaths homeward take our way,
The moon is up, and pours as from an urn
The rich refulgence of her beauteous ray,
No gnarled old trunk, no green and tender spray,
But hath a beauty man shall never paint,
Ambition here may humbly kneel and pray,
A glory folds the earth—free from mortal taint—
Such as the olden painters loved to picture round a
    saint.

The flush of sunset and the gentle eve,
The mellow drooping of the twilight, and
The night, when moon and kindred stars doth weave
A radiant beauty over all the land,
Are pictures fresh from out our Master's hand.
And all have lessons deep within them rife,
Take them unto your hearts, O working band,
They'll buoy ye up and bear ye through earth-strife,
And nerve and fit ye better for the battles of your
    life.

A PAGE FROM LIFE.

FROM the ivied village steeple
  Pealed the joy bells blithe and gay,
And the merry village people
  Thronged the porch in best array,
Why these jovial joy bells swelling
  Through the air afar and wide?
" Oh the lovely Lady Ellen,
  She becomes a happy bride."

Spring then smiled upon the people—
  Spring in all its brightest mood,
But when Autumn tinged that steeple,
  By that same old fane I stood:
Moaned the wind as if a'weary,
  On the road and in the dell;
With a murmur lone and dreary,
  Down the rustling leaflets fell.

The rustic porch was filled with people,
  All with faces white with woe,
And from out the ivied steeple,
  Clanged the solemn church bell slow:
For whom this mournful knelling—
  Who hath renounced life's breath?
" Oh, we bear the Lady Ellen
  To the last sad home of death!"

PAGANINI REDIVIVUS.
(AN ACROSTIC.)

R arest magician, you whose potent spell
C laim'd and entranced a thousand ears to-night,
L ong be it yours to wield the wand so well
E rst borne by HIM. from whose great brow the light
V eered. but to gild you with imperial might,
E arth fading from him—touch, and tone, and thought,
Y ours the strong grasp the falling mantle caught.

TO THE SUMMER WIND.

NOW spreading over
The woodland and glen,
Now fitful rover
Returning again ;
Now coyly dallying
With trees and flowers,
Now madly sallying
To city towers,
Bearing to the lonely maiden,
In the close and silent street,
Breath with scent of flowerets laden,
Flowers her eyes doth pine to greet.

As thou stealest round the basement,
Dreams of past are brought to mind,
And she leaning from her casement,
Blesses thee, O Summer Wind,
Ever shifting and uncertain,
Round the sick one's room ye cling,
Waving back the shading curtain,
Bearing health upon thy wing :
And the old man—nigh a-weary —
As thou sweepest o'er his brow,
Deems the world no longer dreary,
He hath dream of past days now,
Every worldly one must woo thee,
For thou ever art enshrined
With bright thoughts that fly back to thee,
And to childhood, Summer Wind.

Thou hast lingered nigh the palace,
Where all's bud, and breath, and bloom,
Thou hast been where want's pale chalice
Pours o'er homes its meed of doom ;
And we know thou hast been sweeping
O'er the churchyard lone and gray,
And then out to meadows leaping,
Where fair children are at play.
Dashing back the sweeping cluster
From each clear and open brow,
Sending eyes a brighter lustre,
Giving cheeks a richer glow.

Greeting us mid city bustle,
Ah, how sweet to close our eyes.
Hear again the green leaves rustle,
Hear the water's low replies,

Tread once more the winding mazes
Down amid the yellow corn,
Pluck again the meek-eyed daisies,
Sit once more beneath the thorn.
See again bright gardens blooming,
And broad orchards' tempting load,
Riper, richer hues assuming,
Hanging o'er the whitened road.
Join again the merry ramble,
To the woodlands far away,
Be once more amid the gambol,
At the close of summer day.
Hail and welcome, airy comer,
With the bird, and bloom, and bee,
Many a song of childhood's summer
Singest thou, O Wind, to me.

THE MOURNER.

A mourner stood by a lonely grave,
That was almost hid by the grass's wave,
And the trail of flowers that bloomed around,
And flung their scents on the holy ground;
The day was fading, as loath to die,
And a mellow light stole from the gentle sky—
Oh, beautiful hour! oh, beautiful light!
The silver link binding the day to night,
But soberer shadows arose from the wood,
Yet still by the grave that mourner stood;
And the laughter of children came from afar,
But it fell on his ear as a sickening jar,
And the beauties that filled the evening air,
Were as nothing to him in his wild despair—
Despair! for his hopes were overthrown,
And he longed to be with the tenant lone
Of the humble grave that so calmly lay
At his feet, just kissed by the sun's last ray.

    *   *   *   *

He had left her in beauty, in health and bloom,
He came back—she lay in the silent tomb!
What *now* to him that the world was fair,
That flowers flung scent to the balmy air,
That bloom and beauty were all around—
He sighed as he stood on the holy ground,
For the light of his life and his love was dim,
And the world and its beauties were nought to him

THE HUSH OF TWILIGHT.

OH, rose that at the lattice blooms, bid welcome to
  the night,
Rise, full red moon, above the firs, but veil as yet
  thy light;
For in this mystic gloaming hour, we seem to pause
  and stand,
As tho' we saw the star-sprent path that leads to spirit
  land.
Droop thou thy dusky garments, night, yet bring
  thy silv'ry link ;
Oh, river, woo the lilies now, that blossom on thy
  brink.
For voices blending near thy stream, each vow of
  day recalls,
And soft as snow-flake, tenderly, the hush of twilight falls.

Dreams come of other twilights now, the high im-
  perial dome,
Rich with the purple mists that clasp'd the classic
  shrines of Rome,
Again our summer footsteps fall amid green leaves
  and flowers ;
And grand old Rhine land seems to breathe alone
  for us and ours.
Come echoes of the Lurleiberg, the heights of
  Drachenfels,
The sobbing Rhine, each castled crag, once more in
  grandeur swells,
Dreams within dreams, as floats the last low ripple
  on the walls,
And soft as snow-flake, tenderly, the hush of twi-
  light falls.

The shadows gather in the leaves, they glide into
  the room,
And glowing canvas, sculptured stone, grow ghost-
  like in the gloom,
The open vases breathe again rich odours full of
  musk ;
And dead transfigured faces gleam from out the
  silent dusk.
Chords idly struck bring back again, the voices we
  have known,

Dreams come of faded spring-times blent with flush
    of roses blown,
As faint the dying sunset leaves it's ripple on the
    walls,
And soft as snow-flake, tenderly, the hush of twi-
    light falls.

THE STORY OF THE FIRST KING CHARLES.

Epoch, 1640.

STORM CLOUDS.

"I WILL not yield one jot, I am their King
The Lord's anointed, and I *will* be King.
I might have toyed too much at Hampton here
But I e'er thought my people all, were happy and
    content.
And I have led a grave and spotless life,
Nor stooped to ought that might assoil a King.
Go tell to those who would curtail our power
That from my father's self I took the crown
With all its rights and dignities, and these
Will I hand down all unimpaired to him
Who shall succeed me.

                        Further say
That I will call on every loyal heart
That beats in England, aye this realm shall run
With its best blood ere I will swerve or blench.
Go, tell them sirs, I throw the gauntlet down,
If they accept the challenge, on their hands
Be stains of blood, blood that will surely flow
To their eternal shame."

                        So spake the King,
And bowed to those who kneeling kissed his hand;
Then passed he to his barge
Which lay with silken sails and canopies
Upon the tide, his wife and children there.
The oars dipped noiseless, and the vessel moved
Amid a maze of beauty.

                        Odorous June
Had wooed to life her crowning wealth of flowers,
The softest strains of sweetest music stole,
And earth seemed never fairer.

                                        But the King
Was pale and thoughtful, heeding not the swans
In all their snowy beauty hovering round
And lacking guerdons from his royal hand,
A haunting presage, undefined as yet
But hurtling with a presence, could he then
Have seen as others saw, that on the sky
Of his as yet unclouded life, a gloom
Was slowly rising, swift to be a cloud
Fast gathering in its darkness, soon to throw
All England into shadow.

                                        O'er him then.
The arching sky was blue,
But looking round, he marked
Dark clouds were looming, as he stepped
Out at the river stairs, a roll,
Of ominous thunder, shook the summer air.
His palace gates received him,
Pale and thoughtful still.

Epoch. 1642.

WAR.

" For God and King!" the rapid summons ran,
And England's heart flew quivering at the call.
Leaped every shire, unto the Royal Flag,
Flew every loyal sword from loyal sheath.
Each market cross became a rallying point.
Sire vied with son in girding armour on.
Squires brought their yeomen to the trysting place;
Maidens set forth their lovers, gladly forth,
Gay as unto their bridal, kissed were lips,
And kissed the scarves that deftest fingers wove.
" Our King has need, bring out the massive plate.
Huge tankards that have brimmed his royal health,
Rich carved bowls and every dear heir-loom
Pile in the crucible and send the King."

" For God and King " the royal rallying cry.
" For God and England " broke from rebel lips
Set firm as iron with a stern resolve.
And then the roar of battle shook the land.

Many red sunsets saw red dinted heaths,
Many pale moonlights watched the paler dead :
And midnight skies were lighted with the flare

Of burning homesteads, hedgeless fields
Showed where the shock of battle fiercest rolled;
And ever wavering, now the rebel cause
Seemed at its brightest, now the royal camp
Flushed with the blaze of triumph,
Ran with wine, and revelry
Rose up to midnight skies.

Then victory lit upon the Roundhead arms,
And city after city fell, the royal cause
Was slowly fading, then the fight
Of Edgehill shook to shreds the royal ranks,
Until at last the fiercest field of all,
Red Naseby, saw the royal flag
Trailed in the dust, the King a fugitive,
And panting, bruised, and rent
England lay prone under the Roundhead heel.

For "God and King no more,
But "God and England" ran through all the land.

———

Epoch, 1648.

DEATH.

And all is passed!
        Death to the monarch, death.
The fatal axe with edge toward him
Told to all the King must die.
No loyal heart but felt a bitter pang—
No loyal eye but held a wistful tear.
"I fain would see my children ere I die,"
So spake the discrowned monarch, now
He could but sue, when once he could command.
They brought his children to him—one a girl
Just in the blush of maidenhood—a boy
But with the curls of four sad summers
On his baby head. The toy with little tress—
The prayer—the lingering kiss—the last farewell.
The foul night passed. The morning dimly broke,
Heavy, thick-clouded, as though loth to break.
So through the park the mournful pageant moves.
The air is chill and mists are all about.
True to the last a little band
Of those who loved him marked their dying King
And murmured heedless of the Roundhead frown—
"God bless you Sire."

He saw that at his feet
Lay lusty branch just torn from parent tree,
Type of his fate.

Undauntedly he passed
Calm and collected, whilst the prelate shook,
Quivering with anguish, and could scarcely keep
The place of sorrow at his honored side.
So through the hall, when last he'd seen it rich
With lustrous sheen, the crash of music, and
The brave attire of those who pressed
To meet his Kingly glance
All over now, beyond, the scaffold draped
With heaviest black, below, a serried crowd,
No roof, no casement, but was thickly packed ;
The veriest Roundhead must have felt a tinge
Of latent sorrow in that supreme time.
Clashed from the towers, the hours of fullest noon ;
The block—the axe—
A groan from all the crowd—
A blur of shame for ever, on our realm.

1851.

(THE YEAR OF THE GREAT EXHIBITION.)

BRAVELY out from every steeple
Bells, oh gaily clash and chime,
Telling to the list'ning people,
Fast is fleeting Father Time,
That the old year's swiftly dying,
That his race is nearly run,
And that hither gladly hieing
Comes in glory 'FIFTY ONE.

The year that's hastening from us
If but little good has brought,
Brings the new year rich in promise,
That a change shall now be wrought:
Sight unseen by generations,
Who have lived and died before,
It shall see far distant nations
Welcomed by us to our shore.

None are clad in armour warlike,
As they came they come not now,
Only smiling Peace sits starlike,
On each welcome comer's brow,

And as each one seeks his dwelling,
In his far off father land,
Shall his children hear him telling
How we shook him by the hand.

If stern war's offending rattle
Never more is borne on high,
If the last fierce roar of battle,
Hath died on the arching sky.
Holy thoughts shall to thee cling, land,
Unborn nations shall recall,
It was great and glorious England,
First held hand of peace to all.

Be, from now, the sole contentions
To disturb the world wide marts,
Strife, of mutual inventions,
War of sciences and arts,
We can well afford to trample
War, and teach all peace's good,
We have set a bright example,
And we shall be understood.

*   *   *   *

So, as I sit lonely filling
Up the measure of these rhymes,
Hark! I hear the dark air thrilling
With the jovial New Year chimes.
Clash on, bells—yet peal out louder,
Fling abroad our vaunt, our boast,
That a brighter year or prouder
Never dawned upon our coast.

Ring out many an antique error,
Ring in joys that we shall find,
Ring out war, and woe and terror,
Ring in love to all mankind.
By the gathering of the legions
Shall a forward step be won,
And all natives of all regions
HAIL AND BLESS THEE, FIFTY-ONE!

AT THE LOAN EXHIBITION.

I thought there'd be crowding of beauty; the sound
Of a multitude trooping in speed
But with nobody near me, I certainly found
It a *lone* exhibition indeed.

FALLEN LEAVES.

THE Autumn winds are sweeping fast
   Across the distant wold;
The trees are bending to the blast,
   And shake as if a-cold;
A yellow tint of dull decay
   Amid each stout arm weaves,
And in the woods our winding way
   Is strewn with fallen leaves.

Yet once each branch waved broad and fair,
   And glistened bright and high,
And wantoned in the summer air,
   And seemed to mock the sky.
We gazed upon the glossy sheen
   That lit our woodland way,
Nor dreamt, amid the living green,
   Of drooping and decay.

A mother sat her down, and sighed
   For three fair children gone,
Who each had in their beauty died,
   Ere life's first cares came on;
And as I caught her mournful tone
   From out her cottage eaves,
I mused—Alas! life's path is strewn
   Deep, deep with fallen leaves.

HOLMWOOD.

WHO says the spirit of Romance has died,
   Whilst in these deep bosked glens the Autumn
      wakes
   And with its fiercer glory calmly takes
The full flushed splendours from the Summer's side?
Gleam the long vistas now with twin-crowned pride,
   And waters ripple 'mid the wealth of ferns.

In the rich dusk of leaves, where shadows hide,
   Full-thoughted Fancy might in quiet feed,
Sweet Ariel trip in maze of wanton sport,
   Old Pan—yet silent—find his mystic reed,
Titania reign it o'er her merry court,
   And whilst the Autumn moon its glory turns
On sturdy oak, on shadow-haunted yew,
   Puck might out-frolic all his elfin crew.

SONNET.

IT was the flush of a warm summer day,
No fleck of cloud lay on the sky's deep blue,
The ruined church a welcome shadow threw,
And white-sailed ships were twirling far away,
But one faint murmur could our list'ning reach—
A gentle one— the ever restless spray
Bursting its foam-bells on the shingley beach;
And so we sat and read that earnest lay—
The tale of fond, of sweet Evangeline—
And watched her love surviving youth's decay,
Until her wearied spirit floated free.
We're parted now, oh, dearest friend of mine,
But a heart picture this will ever be,
The hour, the book, the ruined church, the low
    sob of the sea.

EVENING LINES.

SEE, Lady! see the sun has sunk,
  The day is nearly gone,
And, like a dusky-sandall'd monk,
  The night is stealing on:
A mellow radiance all the sky
  Has flecked with golden bars,
Save where the evening, silently,
  Illumes it with her stars;
And all is still—in vale, on hill,
  Roams neither bird nor bee;—
Oh, Lady! midst this silence trill
  Some sweet low song to me!
Thanks, Lady, thanks! a charm is wrought
  By thy soft gentle strain,
And chords are stirr'd which I had thought
  Would never wake again.
That song was sung in other days,
  By one of truth and worth,
And with her vanished from my gaze
  The last I loved on earth:
She died just as the gentle spring
  Brought bud and bloom on tree,
Oh, Lady! midst this silence sing
  Once more that song to me!

LINES.

THE gentle light of evening fades,
   And with its golden dye,
Mellows the winding forest glades,
   The watching earth and sky ;
And thou art with me, dearest, thou
   So beautiful and fair,
And falling on thy gentle brow
   It lights a radiance there.

Yet earth may spread her thousand wiles,
   And all her brightness still,
The earth, unhallowed by thy smiles,
   Were cold, and dull, and chill :
But dark the storms of fate may lour,
   And drear the path may be,
Yet, with thy smiles, earth's darkest hour
   Were beautiful to me.

BOTH SIDES.

A man in his carriage was riding along,
   His gaily dressed wife by his side,
In satins and laces she looked like a queen,
   And he like a king in his pride.

A labourer stood in the street as they passed,
   The carriage and couple he eyed,
And he said as he worked with his saw on a log,
   "Oh, I wish I was rich and could ride !"

The man in the carriage remarked to his wife,
   "One thing I would give if I could,
And that's all my wealth for the strength and the
     health
   Of the man who is sawing the wood !"

THE SPANISH PILGRIM.

HO, wanderer from the sunny South—
   Ho, pilgrim from Castile—
Who treads, with proud and haughty glance,
   Our city 'neath thy heel,
Bringing unto our Western eyes
   The blue blood of Madrid,

The triumphs of thy Matadors,
  The glories of thy Cid.
Of purple mists on summer seas,
  The rippling castanet.
Of Maritana's cheek of bloom
  Of Nina's eye of jet—
What time the scented breezes blow
  Through all the summer vines—
What time the gentle light is low
  'Mid Vall'ambrosa's pines—
Come tells us with what ardent thoughts
  Thy strongest pulses leap.
 " Yah ! buy my Spanish onions ?
  One penny !— very cheap !"

SONNET.

PEACE, oh ye scribes, who "babble o' green fields,"
  And rave in song of Summer's soft delight ;
Give me the pleasures merry Winter yields—
  The curtained room—the blazing fire at night.
When the lamp sheds a soft and mellow light,
  And loving eyes are dancing in its rays :
What if without the stern North wind doth bite,
  Frighting weird branches with its vagrant ways?
Within from sweet lips sweetest songs are flowing—
  Lov'd tones that stir a kindred love in us,
Teeming with joy, to this glad season owing—
  These are the lights upon our pathway, thus,
We love old Winter, strain him to our breast,
  And shake him by his horny hand and hail him as
    a guest.

ON THE DEATH OF
LORD RUSSELL.

LOYAL to throne and people, this thy proud
  And well-won guerdon, England's heart shall say,
  Now English earth receive the listless clay
Of one who, toiling, saw the rifting cloud,
  The glimmering dawn : through thickest night the
    day.
Thine was the stern, thine the unbending fight,
When Progress branded Treason, hearts would fail,
  But thou, true Giant-killer, strong in right,
  Rallied the faint hearts : steadfast in thy might,
Girt with high purpose, as with coat of mail.

Well-dinted sword, so nobly sheathed at last ;
  Well-garnered honours, all so proudly won.
  True type of England ! Say, from sire to son,
From all our midst, a loyal heart has passed.

IDLENESS.

FROM all above the solemn firs
  Rise stars and summer moon,
And scarce a wind now wooing stirs
  This languid night of June ;
Full flowered azaleas crown each stalk,
  Down to the sleeping lake,
And blent with roses, flood the walk,
  To-night, deep joyed, we take.

Oh, fountain ! leaping to the night,
  What music in thy song !
Oh, marble statue ! full limbed, white,
  Rich dusk of leaves among ;
Foxglove, fire pillared in thy bloom,
  With pride raise thou thine head ;
And foot pressed grass, thy faint perfume
  Out on the night air shed.

Sheer from a rain of glistening leaves.
  From marge we idly float,
Through maze of water-lily cleaves
  All silently our boat.
Stir, languid breeze of summer, blow,
  Lift soft each scented tress ;
This night life's brightest wine shall flow,
  To love and idleness.

THE BROTHER.

AH, children, as ye gaily stand
    Around your mother's knee,
One link is lost, from your bright band—
    Your brother—where is he?
He comes not now as once he came,
    Your merry meal to share,
Nor join ye in your joyful game,
    Or morn or even prayer.
Yet no need once for him to call,
    His fair and open brow,
And happy looks were first of all,
    Why is he silent now.

CHILDREN.

No more, no more, his merry voice
    Will cheer us in our play,
No more will bid our hearts rejoice,
    For he hath passed away
Twas Autumn—with its many dyes
    The fair old woods were rife—
Our brother turned on us his eyes,
    And spake of hope and life.
Alas, ere blithe birds came along,
    With whispers of the Spring,
He around whom our hopes did throng,
    Was a forgotten thing;
And lost unto the busy crowd,
    But by our household hearth,
Was miss'd the glance so gay and proud,
    The laugh so full of mirth
Was heard no more, but since he hath slept
    Where the grass waves green and high,
His memory in our hearts hath kept
    A place that will not die.